'SHE HAD LIVED BY DELAYS; SHE HAD MEANT TO STOP DRINKING; SHE HAD PUT OFF THE TIME, AND NOW SHE HAD SMASHED HER CAR.'

SAUL BELLOW
Born 1915, Lachine, Canada
Died 2005, Brookline, Massachusetts, USA

'Leaving the Yellow House' first appeared in *Esquire* (January 1958), and was first published in book form in *Mosby's Memoirs and Other Stories*, Viking Press, 1968. It is included in *Collected Stories*, Penguin Modern Classics, 2007.

BELLOW IN PENGUIN MODERN CLASSICS
The Actual
The Adventures of Augie March
Collected Stories
Dangling Man
The Dean's December
Henderson the Rain King
Herzog
Him with His Foot in His Mouth
Humboldt's Gift
It All Adds Up
More Die of Heartbreak
Mr Sammler's Planet
Ravelstein
Seize the Day
To Jerusalem and Back
The Victim

SAUL BELLOW

Leaving the Yellow House

PENGUIN BOOKS

PENGUIN CLASSICS

UK | USA | Canada | Ireland | Australia
India | New Zealand | South Africa

Penguin Books is part of the Penguin Random House group
of companies whose addresses can be found at
global.penguinrandomhouse.com.

This edition first published 2018

008

Copyright © Saul Bellow, 2001

Set in 11.2/13.75 pt Dante MT Std
Typeset by Jouve (UK), Milton Keynes
Printed in Great Britain by Clays Ltd, Elcograf S.p.A.

ISBN: 978-0-241-33899-5

www.greenpenguin.co.uk

The neighbors – there were in all six white people who lived at Sego Desert Lake – told one another that old Hattie could no longer make it alone. The desert life, even with a forced-air furnace in the house and butane gas brought from town in a truck, was still too difficult for her. There were women even older than Hattie in the county. Twenty miles away was Amy Walters, the gold miner's widow. She was a hardy old girl, more wiry and tough than Hattie. Every day of the year she took a bath in the icy lake. And Amy was crazy about money and knew how to manage it, as Hattie did not. Hattie was not exactly a drunkard, but she hit the bottle pretty hard, and now she was in trouble and there was a limit to the help she could expect from even the best of neighbors.

They were fond of her, though. You couldn't help being fond of Hattie. She was big and cheerful, puffy, comic, boastful, with a big round back and stiff, rather long legs. Before the century began she had graduated from finishing school and studied the organ in Paris. But now she didn't know a note from a skillet. She had tantrums when she played canasta. And all that remained of her fine fair hair was frizzled along her forehead in small gray curls. Her forehead was not much wrinkled, but the skin was bluish, the color of skim milk. She walked with long strides in spite of the heaviness of her hips. With her shoulders, she pushed on, round-backed, showing the flat rubber bottoms of her shoes.

Once a week, in the same cheerful, plugging but absent way, she took off her short skirt and the dirty aviator's jacket with the wool collar and put on a girdle, a dress, and high-heeled shoes. When she stood on these heels her fat old body trembled. She wore a big brown Rembrandt-like tam with a ten-cent-store brooch, eyelike, carefully centered. She drew a straight line with lipstick on her mouth, leaving part of the upper lip pale. At the wheel of her old turret-shaped car, she drove, seemingly methodical but speeding dangerously, across forty miles of mountainous desert to buy frozen meat pies and whiskey. She went to the Laundromat and the hairdresser, and then had lunch with two martinis at the Arlington. Afterward she would often visit Marian Nabot's Silvermine Hotel at Miller Street near skid row and pass the rest of the day gossiping and drinking with her cronies, old divorcées like herself who had settled in the West. Hattie never gambled anymore and she didn't care for the movies. And at five o'clock she drove back at the same speed, calmly, partly blinded by the smoke of her cigarette. The fixed cigarette gave her a watering eye.

The Rolfes and the Paces were her only white neighbors at Sego Desert Lake. There was Sam Jervis too, but he was only an old gandy walker who did odd jobs in her garden, and she did not count him. Nor did she count among her neighbors Darly, the dudes' cowboy who worked for the Paces, nor Swede, the telegrapher. Pace had a guest ranch, and Rolfe and his wife were rich and had retired. Thus there were three good houses at the lake, Hattie's yellow house, Pace's, and the Rolfes'. All the rest of the population – Sam, Swede, Watchtah the section foreman, and the Mexicans and Indians and Negroes – lived in shacks and boxcars. There were very few trees, cottonwoods and box elders. Everything else, down to the shores, was sagebrush and juniper. The lake was what remained of an old sea that had covered the volcanic mountains. To the north there were some tungsten mines; to the south, fifteen miles, was an Indian village – shacks built of plywood or railroad ties.

In this barren place Hattie had lived for more than twenty years. Her first summer was spent not in a house but in an Indian wickiup on the shore. She used to say that she had watched the stars from this almost roofless shelter. After her divorce she took up with a cowboy

3

named Wicks. Neither of them had any money – it was the Depression – and they had lived on the range, trapping coyotes for a living. Once a month they would come into town and rent a room and go on a bender. Hattie told this sadly, but also gloatingly, and with many trimmings. A thing no sooner happened to her than it was transformed into something else. 'We were caught in a storm,' she said, 'and we rode hard, down to the lake, and knocked on the door of the yellow house' – now her house. 'Alice Parmenter took us in and let us sleep on the floor.' What had actually happened was that the wind was blowing – there had been no storm – and they were not far from the house anyway; and Alice Parmenter, who knew that Hattie and Wicks were not married, offered them separate beds; but Hattie, swaggering, had said in a loud voice, 'Why get two sets of sheets dirty?' And she and her cowboy had slept in Alice's bed while Alice had taken the sofa.

Then Wicks went away. There was never anybody like him in the sack; he was brought up in a whorehouse and the girls had taught him everything, said Hattie. She didn't really understand what she was saying but believed that she was being Western. More than anything else she wanted to be thought of as a rough, experienced woman of the West. Still, she was a lady, too. She had good silver and good china and engraved stationery, but she kept canned beans and A-1 sauce and tuna fish and bottles of catsup and fruit salad on the library shelves of her living room. On her night table was the Bible her pious brother Angus – the other brother was a heller – had given her; but behind the little door of the commode was a bottle of bourbon. When she awoke in the night she tippled herself back to sleep. In the glove compartment of her old car she kept little sample bottles for emergencies on the road. Old Darly found them after her accident.

The accident did not happen far out in the desert as she had always feared, but very near home. She had had a few martinis with the Rolfes one evening, and as she was driving home over the railroad crossing she lost control of the car and veered off the crossing onto the tracks. The explanation she gave was that she had sneezed, and the sneeze had blinded her and made her twist the wheel. The motor was killed and all four wheels of the car sat smack on the rails. Hattie crept down from the door, high off the roadbed. A great fear took hold of her – for the car, for the future, and not only for the future but spreading back into the past – and she began to hurry on stiff legs through the sagebrush to Pace's ranch.

Now the Paces were away on a hunting trip and had left Darly in charge; he was tending bar in the old cabin that went back to the days of the pony express, when

5

Hattie burst in. There were two customers, a tungsten miner and his girl.

'Darly, I'm in trouble. Help me. I've had an accident,' said Hattie.

How the face of a man will alter when a woman has bad news to tell him! It happened now to lean old Darly; his eyes went flat and looked unwilling, his jaw moved in and out, his wrinkled cheeks began to flush, and he said, 'What's the matter – what's happened to you now?'

'I'm stuck on the tracks. I sneezed. I lost control of the car. Tow me off, Darly. With the pickup. Before the train comes.'

Darly threw down his towel and stamped his high-heeled boots. 'Now what have you gone and done?' he said. 'I told you to stay home after dark.'

'Where's Pace? Ring the fire bell and fetch Pace.'

'There's nobody on the property except me,' said the lean old man. 'And I'm not supposed to close the bar and you know it as well as I do.'

'Please, Darly. I can't leave my car on the tracks.'

'Too bad!' he said. Nevertheless he moved from behind the bar. 'How did you say it happened?'

'I told you, I sneezed,' said Hattie.

Everyone, as she later told it, was as drunk as sixteen thousand dollars: Darly, the miner, and the miner's girl.

Darly was limping as he locked the door of the bar.

A year before, a kick from one of Pace's mares had broken his ribs as he was loading her into the trailer, and he hadn't recovered from it. He was too old. But he dissembled the pain. The high-heeled narrow boots helped, and his painful bending looked like the ordinary stooping posture of a cowboy. However, Darly was not a genuine cowboy, like Pace who had grown up in the saddle. He was a latecomer from the East and until the age of forty had never been on horseback. In this respect he and Hattie were alike. They were not genuine Westerners.

Hattie hurried after him through the ranch yard.

'Damn you!' he said to her. 'I got thirty bucks out of that sucker and I would have skinned him out of his whole paycheck if you minded your business. Pace is going to be sore as hell.'

'You've got to help me. We're neighbors,' said Hattie.

'You're not fit to be living out here. You can't do it anymore. Besides, you're swacked all the time.'

Hattie couldn't afford to talk back. The thought of her car on the tracks made her frantic. If a freight came now and smashed it, her life at Sego Desert Lake would be finished. And where would she go then? She was not fit to live in this place. She had never made the grade at all, only seemed to have made it. And Darly – why did he say such hurtful things to her? Because he himself was

7

sixty-eight years old, and he had no other place to go, either; he took bad treatment from Pace besides. Darly stayed because his only alternative was to go to the soldiers' home. Moreover, the dude women would still crawl into his sack. They wanted a cowboy and they thought he was one. Why, he couldn't even raise himself out of his bunk in the morning. And where else would he get women? 'After the dude season,' she wanted to say to him, 'you always have to go to the Veterans' Hospital to get fixed up again.' But she didn't dare offend him now.

The moon was due to rise. It appeared as they drove over the ungraded dirt road toward the crossing where Hattie's turret-shaped car was sitting on the rails. Driving very fast, Darly wheeled the pickup around, spraying dirt on the miner and his girl, who had followed in their car.

'You get behind the wheel and steer,' Darly told Hattie.

She climbed into the seat. Waiting at the wheel, she lifted up her face and said, 'Please God, I didn't bend the axle or crack the oil pan.'

When Darly crawled under the bumper of Hattie's car the pain in his ribs suddenly cut off his breath, so instead of doubling the tow chain he fastened it at full length. He rose and trotted back to the truck on the tight boots. Motion seemed the only remedy for the pain; not even booze did the trick anymore. He put the pickup into towing gear and began to pull. One side of Hattie's car dropped into the roadbed with a heave of springs. She sat with a stormy, frightened, conscience-stricken face, racing the motor until she flooded it.

The tungsten miner yelled, 'Your chain's too long.'

Hattie was raised high in the air by the pitch of the wheels. She had to roll down the window to let herself out because the door handle had been jammed from inside for years. Hattie struggled out on the uplifted side crying, 'I better call the Swede. I better have him signal. There's a train due.'

'Go on, then,' said Darly. 'You're no good here.'

'Darly, be careful with my car. Be careful.'

The ancient sea bed at this place was flat and low, and the lights of her car and of the truck and of the tungsten miner's Chevrolet were bright and big at twenty miles. Hattie was too frightened to think of this. All she could think was that she was a procrastinating old woman; she had lived by delays; she had meant to stop drinking; she had put off the time, and now she had smashed her car – a terrible end, a terrible judgment on her. She got to the ground and, drawing up her skirt, she started to get over the tow chain. To prove that the chain didn't have to be shortened, and to get the whole thing over with, Darly

9

threw the pickup forward again. The chain jerked up and struck Hattie in the knee and she fell forward and broke her arm.

She cried, 'Darly, Darly, I'm hurt. I fell.'

'The old lady tripped on the chain,' said the miner. 'Back up here and I'll double it for you. You're getting nowheres.'

Drunkenly the miner lay down on his back in the dark, soft red cinders of the roadbed. Darly had backed up to slacken the chain.

Darly hurt the miner, too. He tore some skin from his fingers by racing ahead before the chain was secure. Without complaining, the miner wrapped his hand in his shirttail saying, 'She'll do it now.' The old car came down from the tracks and stood on the shoulder of the road.

'There's your goddamn car,' said Darly to Hattie.

'Is it all right?' she said. Her left side was covered with dirt, but she managed to pick herself up and stand, round-backed and heavy, on her stiff legs. 'I'm hurt, Darly.' She tried to convince him of it.

'Hell if you are,' he said. He believed she was putting on an act to escape blame. The pain in his ribs made him especially impatient with her. 'Christ, if you can't look after yourself anymore you've got no business out here.'

'You're old yourself,' she said. 'Look what you did to me. You can't hold your liquor.'

This offended him greatly. He said, 'I'll take you to the Rolfes. They let you booze it up in the first place, so let them worry about you. I'm tired of your bunk, Hattie.'

He raced uphill. Chains, spade, and crowbar clashed on the sides of the pickup. She was frightened and held her arm and cried. Rolfe's dogs jumped at her to lick her when she went through the gate. She shrank from them crying, 'Down, down.'

'Darly,' she cried in the darkness, 'take care of my car. Don't leave it standing there on the road. Darly, take care of it, please.'

But Darly in his ten-gallon hat, his chin-bent face wrinkled, small and angry, a furious pain in his ribs, tore away at high speed.

'Oh, God, what will I do,' she said.

The Rolfes were having a last drink before dinner, sitting at their fire of pitchy railroad ties, when Hattie opened the door. Her knee was bleeding, her eyes were tiny with shock, her face gray with dust.

'I'm hurt,' she said desperately. 'I had an accident. I sneezed and lost control of the wheel. Jerry, look after the car. It's on the road.'

They bandaged her knee and took her home and put her to bed. Helen Rolfe wrapped a heating pad around her arm.

'I can't have the pad,' Hattie complained. 'The switch

goes on and off, and every time it does it starts my generator and uses up the gas.'

'Ah, now, Hattie,' Rolfe said, 'this is not the time to be stingy. We'll take you to town in the morning and have you looked over. Helen will phone Dr Stroud.'

Hattie wanted to say, 'Stingy! Why you're the stingy ones. I just haven't got anything. You and Helen are ready to hit each other over two bits in canasta.' But the Rolfes were good to her; they were her only real friends here. Darly would have let her lie in the yard all night, and Pace would have sold her to the bone man. He'd give her to the knacker for a buck.

So she didn't talk back to the Rolfes, but as soon as they left the yellow house and walked through the super-clear moonlight under the great skirt of box-elder shadows to their new station wagon, Hattie turned off the switch, and the heavy swirling and battering of the generator stopped. Presently she became aware of real pain, deeper pain, in her arm, and she sat rigid, warming the injured place with her hand. It seemed to her that she could feel the bone sticking out. Before leaving, Helen Rolfe had thrown over her a comforter that had belonged to Hattie's dead friend India, from whom she had inherited the small house and everything in it. Had the comforter lain on India's bed the night she died? Hattie tried to remember, but her thoughts were mixed up. She was fairly sure the deathbed pillow was in the loft, and she believed she had put the death bedding in a trunk. Then how had this comforter got out? She couldn't do anything about it now but draw it away from contact with her skin. It kept her legs warm. This she accepted, but she didn't want it any nearer.

More and more Hattie saw her own life as though, from birth to the present, every moment had been filmed. Her fancy was that when she died she would see the film in the next world. Then she would know how she had appeared from the back, watering the plants, in the bathroom, asleep, playing the organ, embracing – everything, even tonight, in pain, almost the last pain, perhaps, for she couldn't take much more. How many twists and angles had life to show her yet? There couldn't be much film left. To lie awake and think such thoughts was the worst thing in the world. Better death than insomnia. Hattie not only loved sleep, she believed in it.

The first attempt to set the bone was not successful. 'Look what they've done to me,' said Hattie and showed visitors the discolored breast. After the second operation her mind wandered. The sides of her bed had to be raised, for in her delirium she roamed the wards. She cursed at the nurses when they shut her in. 'You can't make people prisoners in a democracy without a trial, you bitches.'

She had learned from Wicks how to swear. '*He* was profane,' she used to say. 'I picked it up unconsciously.'

For several weeks her mind was not clear. Asleep, her face was lifeless; her cheeks were puffed out and her mouth, no longer wide and grinning, was drawn round and small. Helen sighed when she saw her.

'Shall we get in touch with her family?' Helen asked the doctor. His skin was white and thick. He had chestnut hair, abundant but very dry. He sometimes explained to his patients, 'I had a tropical disease during the war.'

He asked, 'Is there a family?'

'Old brothers. Cousins' children,' said Helen. She tried to think who would be called to her own bedside (she was old enough for that). Rolfe would see that she was cared for. He would hire private nurses. Hattie could not afford that. She had already gone beyond her means. A trust company in Philadelphia paid her eighty dollars a month. She had a small savings account.

'I suppose it'll be up to us to get her out of hock,' said Rolfe. 'Unless the brother down in Mexico comes across. We may have to phone one of those old guys.'

In the end, no relations had to be called. Hattie began to recover. At last she could recognize visitors, though her mind was still in disorder. Much that had happened she couldn't recall.

'How many quarts of blood did they have to give me?' she kept asking. 'I seem to remember five, six, eight different transfusions. Daylight, electric light . . .' She tried to smile, but she couldn't make a pleasant face as yet. 'How am I going to pay?' she said. 'At twenty-five bucks a quart. My little bit of money is just about wiped out.'

Blood became her constant topic, her preoccupation. She told everyone who came to see her, '– have to replace all that blood. They poured gallons into me. Gallons. I hope it was all good.' And, though very weak, she began to grin and laugh again. There was more hissing in her laughter than formerly; the illness had affected her chest.

'No cigarettes, no booze,' the doctor told Helen.

'Doctor,' Helen asked him, 'do you expect her to change?'

'All the same, I am obliged to say it.'

'Life sober may not be much of a temptation to her,' said Helen.

Her husband laughed. When Rolfe's laughter was intense it blinded one of his eyes. His short Irish face turned red; on the bridge of his small, sharp nose the skin whitened. 'Hattie's like me,' he said. 'She'll be in business till she's cleaned out. And if Sego Lake turned to whisky she'd use her last strength to knock her old yellow house down to build a raft of it. She'd float away on whisky. So why talk temperance?'

Hattie recognized the similarity between them. When he came to see her she said, 'Jerry, you're the only one I can really talk to about my troubles. What am I going to do for money? I have Hotchkiss Insurance. I paid eight dollars a month.'

'That won't do you much good, Hat. No Blue Cross?'

'I let it drop ten years ago. Maybe I could sell some of my valuables.'

'What valuables have you got?' he said. His eye began to droop with laughter.

'Why,' she said defiantly, 'there's plenty. First there's the beautiful, precious Persian rug that India left me.'

'Coals from the fireplace have been burning it for years, Hat!'

'The rug is in *perfect* condition,' she said with an angry sway of the shoulders. 'A beautiful object like that never loses its value. And the oak table from the Spanish monastery is three hundred years old.'

'With luck you could get twenty bucks for it. It would cost fifty to haul it out of here. It's the house you ought to sell.'

'The house?' she said. Yes, that had been in her mind. 'I'd have to get twenty thousand for it.'

'Eight is a fair price.'

'Fifteen . . .' She was offended, and her voice recovered its strength. 'India put eight into it in two years. And don't forget that Sego Lake is one of the most beautiful places in the world.'

'But where is it? Five hundred and some miles to San Francisco and two hundred to Salt Lake City. Who wants to live way out here but a few eccentrics like you and India? And me?'

'There are things you can't put a price tag on. Beautiful things.'

'Oh, bull, Hattie! You don't know squat about beautiful things. Any more than I do. I live here because it figures for me, and you because India left you the house. And just in the nick of time, too. Without it you wouldn't have had a pot of your own.'

His words offended Hattie; more than that, they frightened her. She was silent and then grew thoughtful, for she was fond of Jerry Rolfe and he of her. He had good sense and, moreover, he only expressed her own thoughts. He spoke no more than the truth about India's death and the house. But she told herself, He doesn't know everything. You'd have to pay a San Francisco architect ten thousand just to *think* of such a house. Before he drew a line.

'Jerry,' the old woman said, 'what am I going to do about replacing the blood in the blood bank?'

'Do you want a quart from me, Hat?' His eye began to fall shut.

17

'You won't do. You had that tumor, two years ago. I think Darly ought to give some.'

'The old man?' Rolfe laughed at her. 'You want to kill him?'

'Why!' said Hattie with anger, lifting up her massive face. Fever and perspiration had frayed the fringe of curls; at the back of the head the hair had knotted and matted so that it had to be shaved. 'Darly almost killed me. It's his fault that I'm in this condition. He must have *some* blood in him. He runs after all the chicks – all of them – young and old.'

'Come, you were drunk, too,' said Rolfe.

'I've driven drunk for forty years. It was the sneeze. Oh, Jerry, I feel wrung out,' said Hattie, haggard, sitting forward in bed. But her face was cleft by her nonsensically happy grin. She was not one to be miserable for long; she had the expression of a perennial survivor.

Every other day she went to the therapist. The young woman worked her arm for her; it was a pleasure and a comfort to Hattie, who would have been glad to leave the whole cure to her. However, she was given other exercises to do, and these were not so easy. They rigged a pulley for her and Hattie had to hold both ends of a rope and saw it back and forth through the scraping little wheel. She bent heavily from the hips and coughed over her cigarette. But the most important exercise of all she shirked. This required her to put the flat of her hand to the wall at the level of her hips and, by working her finger tips slowly, to make the hand ascend to the height of her shoulder. That was painful; she often forgot to do it, although the doctor warned her, 'Hattie, you don't want adhesions, do you?'

A light of despair crossed Hattie's eyes. Then she said, 'Oh, Dr Stroud, buy my house from me.'

'I'm a bachelor. What would I do with a house?'

'I know just the girl for you – my cousin's daughter. Perfectly charming and very brainy. Just about got her PhD.'

'You must get quite a few proposals yourself,' said the doctor.

'From crazy desert rats. They chase me. But,' she said, 'after I pay my bills I'll be in pretty punk shape. If at least I could replace that blood in the blood bank I'd feel easier.'

'If you don't do as the therapist tells you, Hattie, you'll need another operation. Do you know what adhesions are?'

She knew. But Hattie thought, *How long must I go on taking care of myself?* It made her angry to hear him speak of another operation. She had a moment of panic, but she covered it up. With him, this young man whose skin

19

was already as thick as buttermilk and whose chestnut hair was as dry as death, she always assumed the part of a child. In a small voice she said, 'Yes, doctor.' But her heart was in a fury.

Night and day, however, she repeated, 'I was in the Valley of the Shadow. But I'm alive.' She was weak, she was old, she couldn't follow a train of thought very easily, she felt faint in the head. But she was still here; here was her body, it filled space, a great body. And though she had worries and perplexities, and once in a while her arm felt as though it was about to give her the last stab of all; and though her hair was scrappy and old, like onion roots, and scattered like nothing under the comb, yet she sat and amused herself with visitors; her great grin split her face; her heart warmed with every kind word.

And she thought, People will help me out. It never did me any good to worry. At the last minute something turned up, when I wasn't looking for it. Marian loves me. Helen and Jerry love me. Half Pint loves me. They would never let me go to the ground. And I love them. If it were the other way around, I'd never let them go down.

Above the horizon, in a baggy vastness which Hattie by herself occasionally visited, the features of India, her *shade*, sometimes rose. India was indignant and scolding. Not mean. Not really mean. Few people had ever been really mean to Hattie. But India was annoyed with her. 'The garden is going to hell, Hattie,' she said. 'Those lilac bushes are all shriveled.'

'But what can I do? The hose is rotten. It broke. It won't reach.'

'Then dig a trench,' said the phantom of India. 'Have old Sam dig a trench. But save the bushes.'

Am I thy servant still? said Hattie to herself. *No*, she thought, *let the dead bury their dead.*

But she didn't defy India now any more than she had done when they lived together. Hattie was supposed to keep India off the bottle, but often both of them began to get drunk after breakfast. They forgot to dress, and in their slips the two of them wandered drunkenly around the house and blundered into each other, and they were in despair at having been so weak. Late in the afternoon they would be sitting in the living room, waiting for the sun to set. It shrank, burning itself out on the crumbling edges of the mountains. When the sun passed, the fury of the daylight ended and the mountain surfaces were more blue, broken, like cliffs of coal. They no longer suggested faces. The east began to look simple, and the lake less inhuman and haughty. At last India would say, 'Hattie – it's time for the lights.' And Hattie would pull the switch chains of the lamps, several of them, to give the generator a good shove. She would turn on some of the wobbling eighteenth-century-style lamps whose shades stood out from their slender bodies like dragon-flies' wings. The little engine in the shed would shuffle, then spit, then charge and bang, and the first weak light would rise unevenly in the bulbs.

'Hettie!' cried India. After she drank she was penitent, but her penitence too was a hardship to Hattie, and the worse her temper the more British her accent became. '*Where the hell ah you Het-tie!*' After India's death Hattie found some poems she had written in which she, Hattie, was affectionately and even touchingly mentioned. That was a good thing – Literature. Education. Breeding. But Hattie's interest in ideas was very small, whereas India had been all over the world. India was used to brilliant society. India wanted her to discuss Eastern religion, Bergson and Proust, and Hattie had no head for this, and so India blamed her drinking on Hattie. 'I can't talk to you,' she would say. 'You don't understand religion or culture. And I'm here because I'm not fit to be anywhere else. I can't live in New York anymore. It's too dangerous for a woman my age to be drunk in the street at night.'

And Hattie, talking to her Western friends about India, would say, 'She is a lady' (implying that they made a pair). 'She is a creative person' (this was why they found each other so congenial). 'But helpless? Completely. Why she can't even get her own girdle on.'

'Hettie! Come here. Het-tie! Do you know what sloth is?'

Undressed, India sat on her bed and with the cigarette in her drunken, wrinkled, ringed hand she burned holes in the blankets. On Hattie's pride she left many small scars, too. She treated her like a servant.

Weeping, India begged Hattie afterward to forgive her. *'Hettie, please don't condemn me in your heart. Forgive me, dear, I know I am bad. But I hurt myself more in my evil than I hurt you.'*

Hattie would keep a stiff bearing. She would lift up her face with its incurved nose and puffy eyes and say, 'I am a Christian person. I never bear a grudge.' And by repeating this she actually brought herself to forgive India.

But of course Hattie had no husband, no child, no skill, no savings. And what she would have done if India had not died and left her the yellow house nobody knows.

Jerry Rolfe said privately to Hattie's friend Marian, a businesswoman in town, 'Hattie can't do anything for herself. If I hadn't been around during the forty-four blizzard she and India both would have starved. She's always been careless and lazy and now she can't even chase a cow out of the yard. She's too feeble. The thing for her to do is to go east to her damn brother. Hattie would have ended at the poor farm if it hadn't been for India.

But besides the damn house India should have left her some dough. She didn't use her goddamn head.'

When Hattie returned to the lake she stayed with the Rolfes. 'Well, old shellback,' said Jerry, 'there's a little more life in you now.'

Indeed, with joyous eyes, the cigarette in her mouth and her hair newly frizzed and overhanging her forehead, she seemed to have triumphed again. She was pale, but she grinned, she chuckled, and she held a bourbon old-fashioned with a cherry and a slice of orange in it. She was on rations; the Rolfes allowed her two a day. Her back, Helen noted, was more bent than before. Her knees went outward a little weakly; her feet, however, came close together at the ankles.

'Oh, Helen dear and Jerry dear, I am so thankful, so glad to be back at the lake. I can look after my place again, and I'm here to see the spring. It's more gorgeous than ever.'

Heavy rains had fallen while Hattie was away. The sego lilies, which bloomed only after a wet winter, came up from the loose dust, especially around the marl pit; but even on the burnt granite they seemed to grow. Desert peach was beginning to appear, and in Hattie's yard the rosebushes were filling out. The roses were yellow and abundant, and the odor they gave off was like that of damp tea leaves.

'Before it gets hot enough for the rattlesnakes,' said Hattie to Helen, 'we ought to drive up to Marky's ranch and gather watercress.'

Hattie was going to attend to lots of things, but the heat came early that year and, as there was no television to keep her awake, she slept most of the day. She was now able to dress herself, though there was little more that she could do. Sam Jervis rigged the pulley for her on the porch and she remembered once in a while to use it. Mornings when she had her strength she rambled over to her own house, examining things, being important and giving orders to Sam Jervis and Wanda Gingham. At ninety, Wanda, a Shoshone, was still an excellent seamstress and housecleaner.

Hattie looked over the car, which was parked under a cottonwood tree. She tested the engine. Yes, the old pot would still go. Proudly, happily, she listened to the noise of tappets; the dry old pipe shook as the smoke went out at the rear. She tried to work the shift, turn the wheel. That, as yet, she couldn't do. But it would come soon, she was confident.

At the back of the house the soil had caved in a little over the cesspool and a few of the old railroad ties over the top had rotted. Otherwise things were in good shape. Sam had looked after the garden. He had fixed a new catch for the gate after Pace's horses – maybe because he

25

could never afford to keep them in hay – had broken in and Sam found them grazing and drove them out. Luckily, they hadn't damaged many of her plants. Hattie felt a moment of wild rage against Pace. He had brought the horses into her garden for a free feed, she was sure. But her anger didn't last long. It was reabsorbed into the feeling of golden pleasure that enveloped her. She had little strength, but all that she had was a pleasure to her. So she forgave even Pace, who would have liked to do her out of the house, who had always used her, embarrassed her, cheated her at cards, swindled her. All that he did he did for the sake of his quarter horses. He was a fool about horses. They were ruining him. Racing horses was a millionaire's amusement.

She saw his animals in the distance, feeding. Unsaddled, the mares appeared undressed; they reminded her of naked women walking with their glossy flanks in the sego lilies which curled on the ground. The flowers were yellowish, like winter wool, but fragrant; the mares, naked and gentle, walked through them. Their strolling, their perfect beauty, the sound of their hoofs on stone touched a deep place in Hattie's nature. Her love for horses, birds, and dogs was well known. Dogs led the list. And now a piece cut from a green blanket reminded Hattie of her dog Richie. The blanket was one he had torn, and she had cut it into strips and placed them under the doors to keep out the drafts. In the house she found more traces of him: hair he had shed on the furniture. Hattie was going to borrow Helen's vacuum cleaner, but there wasn't really enough current to make it pull as it should. On the doorknob of India's room hung the dog collar.

Hattie had decided that she would have herself moved into India's bed when it was time to die. Why should there be two deathbeds? A perilous look came into her eyes, her lips were pressed together forbiddingly. *I follow*, she said, speaking to India with an inner voice, *so never mind*. Presently – before long – she would have to leave the yellow house in her turn. And as she went into the parlor, thinking of the will, she sighed. Pretty soon she would have to attend to it. India's lawyer, Claiborne, helped her with such things. She had phoned him in town, while she was staying with Marian, and talked matters over with him. He had promised to try to sell the house for her. Fifteen thousand was her bottom price, she said. If he couldn't find a buyer, perhaps he could find a tenant. Two hundred dollars a month was the rental she set. Rolfe laughed. Hattie turned toward him one of those proud, dulled looks she always took on when he angered her. Haughtily she said, 'For summer on Sego Lake? That's reasonable.'

'You're competing with Pace's ranch.'

'Why, the food is stinking down there. And he cheats the dudes,' said Hattie. 'He really cheats them at cards. You'll never catch me playing blackjack with him again.'

And what would she do, thought Hattie, if Claiborne could neither rent nor sell the house? This question she shook off as regularly as it returned. *I don't have to be a burden on anybody*, thought Hattie. *It's looked bad many a time before, but when push came to shove, I made it. Somehow I got by.* But she argued with herself: *How many times? How long, O God – an old thing, feeble, no use to anyone?* Who said she had any right to own property?

She was sitting on her sofa, which was very old – India's sofa – eight feet long, kidney-shaped, puffy, and bald. An underlying pink shone through the green; the upholstered tufts were like the pads of dogs' paws; between them rose bunches of hair. Here Hattie slouched, resting, with knees wide apart and a cigarette in her mouth, eyes half shut but farseeing. The mountains seemed not fifteen miles but fifteen hundred feet away, the lake a blue band; the tealike odor of the roses, though they were still unopened, was already in the air, for Sam was watering them in the heat. Gratefully Hattie yelled, 'Sam!'

Sam was very old, and all shanks. His feet looked big. His old railroad jacket was made tight across the back by his stoop. A crooked finger with its great broad nail over the mouth of the hose made the water spray and sparkle. Happy to see Hattie, he turned his long jaw, empty of teeth, and his long blue eyes, which seemed to bend back to penetrate into his temples (it was his face that turned, not his body), and he said, 'Oh, there, Hattie. You've made it home today? Welcome, Hattie.'

'Have a beer, Sam. Come around the kitchen door and I'll give you a beer.'

She never had Sam in the house, owing to his skin disease. There were raw patches on his chin and behind his ears. Hattie feared infection from his touch, having decided that he had impetigo. She gave him the beer can, never a glass, and she put on gloves before she used the garden tools. Since he would take no money from her – Wanda Gingham charged a dollar a day – she got Marian to find old clothes for him in town and she left food for him at the door of the damp-wood-smelling boxcar where he lived.

'How's the old wing, Hat?' he said.

'It's coming. I'll be driving the car again before you know it,' she told him. 'By the first of May I'll be driving again.' Every week she moved the date forward. 'By Decoration Day I expect to be on my own again,' she said.

In mid-June, however, she was still unable to drive. Helen Rolfe said to her, 'Hattie, Jerry and I are due in Seattle the first week of July.'

'Why, you never told me that,' said Hattie.

'You don't mean to tell me this is the first you heard of it,' said Helen. 'You've known about it from the first – since Christmas.'

It wasn't easy for Hattie to meet her eyes. She presently put her head down. Her face became very dry, especially the lips. 'Well, don't you worry about me. I'll be all right here,' she said.

'Who's going to look after you?' said Jerry. He evaded nothing himself and tolerated no evasion in others. Except that, as Hattie knew, he made every possible allowance for her. But who would help her? She couldn't count on her friend Half Pint, she couldn't really count on Marian either. She had had only the Rolfes to turn to. Helen, trying to be steady, gazed at her and made sad, involuntary movements with her head, sometimes nodding, sometimes seeming as if she disagreed. Hattie, with her inner voice, swore at her: *Bitch-eyes. I can't make it the way she does because I'm old. Is that fair?* And yet she admired Helen's eyes. Even the skin about them, slightly wrinkled, heavy underneath, was touching, beautiful. There was a heaviness in her bust that went, as if by attachment, with the heaviness of her eyes. Her head, her hands and feet should have taken a more slender body. Helen, said Hattie, was the nearest thing she had on earth to a sister. But there was no reason to go to

Seattle – no genuine business. Why the hell Seattle? It was only idleness, only a holiday. The only reason was Hattie herself; this was their way of telling her that there was a limit to what she could expect them to do for her. Helen's nervous head wavered, but her thoughts were steady. She knew what was passing through Hattie's mind. Like Hattie, she was an idle woman. Why was her right to idleness better?

Because of money? thought Hattie. Because of age? Because she has a husband? Because she had a daughter in Swarthmore College? But an interesting thing occurred to her. Helen disliked being idle, whereas Hattie herself had never made any bones about it: an idle life was all she was good for. But for her it had been uphill all the way, because when Waggoner divorced her she didn't have a cent. She even had to support Wicks for seven or eight years. Except with horses, Wicks had no sense. And then she had had to take tons of dirt from India. *I am the one*, Hattie asserted to herself. *I would know what to do with Helen's advantages. She only suffers from them. And if she wants to stop being an idle woman why can't she start with me, her neighbor?* Hattie's skin, for all its puffiness, burned with anger. She said to Rolfe and Helen, 'Don't worry. I'll make out. But if I have to leave the lake you'll be ten times more lonely than before. Now I'm going back to my house.'

She lifted up her broad old face, and her lips were childlike with suffering. She would never take back what she had said.

But the trouble was no ordinary trouble. Hattie was herself aware that she rambled, forgot names, and answered when no one spoke.

'We can't just take charge of her,' Rolfe said. 'What's more, she ought to be near a doctor. She keeps her shotgun loaded so she can fire it if anything happens to her in the house. But who knows what she'll shoot? I don't believe it was Jacamares who killed that Doberman of hers.'

Rolfe drove into the yard the day after she moved back to the yellow house and said, 'I'm going into town. I can bring you some chow if you like.'

She couldn't afford to refuse his offer, angry though she was, and she said, 'Yes, bring me some stuff from the Mountain Street Market. Charge it.' She had only some frozen shrimp and a few cans of beer in the icebox. When Rolfe had gone she put out the package of shrimp to thaw.

People really used to stick by one another in the West. Hattie now saw herself as one of the pioneers. The modern breed had come later. After all, she had lived on the range like an old-timer. Wicks had had to shoot their Christmas dinner and she had cooked it – venison. He killed it on the reservation, and if the Indians had caught them, there would have been hell to pay.

The weather was hot, the clouds were heavy and calm in a large sky. The horizon was so huge that in it the lake must have seemed like a saucer of milk. *Some milk!* Hattie thought. Two thousand feet down in the middle, so deep no corpse could ever be recovered. A body, they said, went around with the currents. And there were rocks like eyeteeth, and hot springs, and colorless fish at the bottom which were never caught. Now that the white pelicans were nesting they patrolled the rocks for snakes and other egg thieves. They were so big and flew so slow you might imagine they were angels. Hattie no longer visited the lake shore; the walk exhausted her. She saved her strength to go to Pace's bar in the afternoon.

She took off her shoes and stockings and walked on bare feet from one end of her house to the other. On the land side she saw Wanda Gingham sitting near the tracks while her great-grandson played in the soft red gravel. Wanda wore a large purple shawl and her black head was bare. All about her was – was nothing, Hattie thought; for she had taken a drink, breaking her rule. Nothing her mountains, thrust out like men's bodies; the sagebrush was the hair on their chests.

The warm wind blew dust from the marl pit. This

white powder made her sky less blue. On the water side were the pelicans, pure as spirits, slow as angels, blessing the air as they flew with great wings.

Should she or should she not have Sam do something about the vine on the chimney? Sparrows nested in it, and she was glad of that. But all summer long the king snakes were after them and she was afraid to walk in the garden. When the sparrows scratched the ground for seed they took a funny bound; they held their legs stiff and flung back the dust with both feet. Hattie sat down at her old Spanish monastery table, watching them in the cloudy warmth of the day, clasping her hands, chuckling and sad. The bushes were crowded with yellow roses, half of them now rotted. The lizards scrambled from shadow to shadow. The water was smooth as air, gaudy as silk. The mountains succumbed, falling asleep in the heat. Drowsy, Hattie lay down on her sofa, its pads to her always like dogs' paws. She gave in to sleep and when she woke it was midnight; she did not want to alarm the Rolfes by putting on her lights, so she took advantage of the moon to eat a few thawed shrimps and go to the bathroom. She undressed and lifted herself into bed and lay there feeling her sore arm. Now she knew how much she missed her dog. The whole matter of the dog weighed heavily on her soul. She came close to tears, thinking about him, and she went to sleep oppressed by her secret.

I suppose I had better try to pull myself together a little, thought Hattie nervously in the morning. *I can't just sleep my way through.* She knew what her difficulty was. Before any serious question her mind gave way. It scattered or diffused. She said to herself, *I can see bright, but I feel dim. I guess I'm not so lively anymore. Maybe I'm becoming a little touched in the head, as Mother was.* But she was not so old as her mother was when she did those strange things. At eighty-five, her mother had to be kept from going naked in the street. *I'm not as bad as that yet. Thank God! Yes, I walked into the men's wards, but that was when I had a fever, and my nightie was on.*

She drank a cup of Nescafé and it strengthened her determination to do something for herself. In all the world she had only her brother Angus to go to. Her brother Will had led a rough life; he was an old heller, and now he drove everyone away. He was too crabby, thought Hattie. Besides he was angry because she had lived so long with Wicks. Angus would forgive her. But then he and his wife were not her kind. With them she couldn't drink, she couldn't smoke, she had to make herself small-mouthed, and she would have to wait while they read a chapter of the Bible before breakfast. Hattie could not bear to sit at table waiting for meals. Besides, she had a house of her own at last. Why should she have to leave it? She had never owned a thing before. And now she was not allowed to enjoy her yellow house. *But I'll keep it*, she said to herself rebelliously. *I swear to God I'll keep it. Why, I barely just got it. I haven't had time.* And she went out on the porch to work the pulley and do something about the adhesions in her arm. She was sure now that they were there. *And what will I do?* she cried to herself. *What will I do? Why did I ever go to Rolfe's that night – and why did I lose control on the crossing?* She couldn't say, now, 'I sneezed.' She couldn't even remember what had happened, except that she saw the boulders and the twisting blue rails and Darly. It was Darly's fault. He was sick and old himself. *He* couldn't make it. He envied her the house, and her woman's peaceful life. Since she returned from the hospital he hadn't even come to visit her. He only said, 'Hell, I'm sorry for her, but it was her fault.' What hurt him most was that she had said he couldn't hold his liquor.

Fierceness, swearing to God did no good. She was still the same procrastinating old woman. She had a letter to answer from Hotchkiss Insurance and it drifted out of sight. She was going to phone Claiborne the lawyer, but it slipped her mind. One morning she announced to Helen that she believed she would apply to an institution in Los Angeles that took over the property of old people and managed it for them. They gave you an apartment right on the ocean, and your meals and medical care. You had to sign over half of your estate. 'It's fair enough,' said Hattie. 'They take a gamble. I may live to be a hundred.'

'I wouldn't be surprised,' said Helen.

However, Hattie never got around to sending to Los Angeles for the brochure. But Jerry Rolfe took it on himself to write a letter to her brother Angus about her condition. And he drove over also to have a talk with Amy Walters, the gold miner's widow at Fort Walters – as the ancient woman called it. The fort was an old tar-paper building over the mine. The shaft made a cess-pool unnecessary. Since the death of her second husband no one had dug for gold. On a heap of stones near the road a crimson sign FORT WALTERS was placed. Behind it was a flagpole. The American flag was raised every day.

Amy was working in the garden in one of dead Bill's shirts. Bill had brought water down from the mountains for her in a homemade aqueduct so she could raise her own peaches and vegetables.

'Amy,' Rolfe said, 'Hattie's back from the hospital and living all alone. You have no folks and neither has she. Not to beat around the bush about it, why don't you live together?'

Amy's face had great delicacy. Her winter baths in the lake, her vegetable soups, the waltzes she played for herself alone on the grand piano that stood beside her woodstove, the murder stories she read till darkness obliged her to close the book – this life of hers had made her remote. She looked delicate, yet there was no way to affect her composure, she couldn't be touched. It was very strange.

'Hattie and me have different habits, Jerry,' said Amy. 'And Hattie wouldn't like my company. I can't drink with her. I'm a teetotaler.'

'That's true,' said Rolfe, recalling that Hattie referred to Amy as if she were a ghost. He couldn't speak to Amy of the solitary death in store for her. There was not a cloud in the arid sky today, and there was no shadow of death on Amy. She was tranquil, she seemed to be supplied with a sort of pure fluid that would feed her life slowly for years to come.

He said, 'All kinds of things could happen to a woman like Hattie in that yellow house, and nobody would know.'

'That's a fact. She doesn't know how to take care of herself.'

'She can't. Her arm hasn't healed.'

Amy didn't say that she was sorry to hear it. In the place of those words came a silence which might have meant that. Then she said, 'I might go over there a few hours a day, but she would have to pay me.'

'Now, Amy, you must know as well as I do that Hattie

has no money – not much more than her pension. Just the house.'

At once Amy said, no pause coming between his words and hers, 'I would take care of her if she'd agree to leave the house to me.'

'Leave it in your hands, you mean?' said Rolfe. 'To manage?'

'In her will. To belong to me.'

'Why, Amy, what would you do with Hattie's house?' he said.

'It would be my property, that's all. I'd have it.'

'Maybe you would leave Fort Walters to her in your will,' he said.

'Oh, no,' she said. 'Why should I? I'm not asking Hattie for her help. I don't need it. Hattie is a city woman.'

Rolfe could not carry this proposal back to Hattie. He was too wise ever to mention her will to her.

But Pace was not so careful of her feelings. By mid-June Hattie had begun to visit his bar regularly. She had so many things to think about she couldn't stay at home. When Pace came in from the yard one day – he had been packing the wheels of his horse trailer and was wiping grease from his fingers – he said with his usual bluntness, 'How would you like it if I paid you fifty bucks a month for the rest of your life, Hat?'

Hattie was holding her second old-fashioned of the day. At the bar she made it appear that she observed the limit; but she had started drinking at home. One before lunch, one during, one after lunch. She began to grin, expecting Pace to make one of his jokes. But he was wearing his scoop-shaped Western hat as level as a Quaker, and he had drawn down his chin, a sign that he was not fooling. She said, 'That would be nice, but what's the catch?'

'No catch,' he said. 'This is what we'd do. I'd give you five hundred dollars cash, and fifty bucks a month for life, and you let me sleep some dudes in the yellow house, and you'd leave the house to me in your will.'

'What kind of a deal is that?' said Hattie, her look changing. 'I thought we were friends.'

'It's the best deal you'll ever get,' he said.

The weather was sultry, but Hattie till now had thought that it was nice. She had been dreamy but comfortable, about to begin to enjoy the cool of the day; but now she felt that such cruelty and injustice had been waiting to attack her, that it would have been better to die in the hospital than be so disillusioned.

She cried, 'Everybody wants to push me out. You're a cheater, Pace. God! I know you. Pick on somebody else. Why do you have to pick on me? Just because I happen to be around?'

'Why, no, Hattie,' he said, trying now to be careful. 'It was just a business offer.'

'Why don't you give me some blood for the bank if you're such a friend of mine?'

'Well, Hattie, you drink too much and you oughtn't to have been driving anyway.'

'I sneezed, and you know it. The whole thing happened because I sneezed. Everybody knows that. I wouldn't sell you my house. I'd give it away to the lepers first. You'd let me go away and never send me a cent. You never pay anybody. You can't even buy wholesale in town anymore because nobody trusts you. I'm stuck, that's all, just stuck. I keep on saying that this is my only home in all the world, this is where my friends are, and the weather is always perfect and the lake is beautiful. But I wish the whole damn empty old place were in hell. It's not human and neither are you. But I'll be here the day the sheriff takes away your horses – you never mind! I'll be clapping and applauding!'

He told her then that she was drunk again, and so she was, but she was more than that, and though her head was spinning she decided to go back to the house at once and take care of some things she had been putting off. This very day she was going to write to the lawyer, Claiborne, and make sure that Pace never got her property.

She wouldn't put it past him to swear in court that India had promised him the yellow house.

She sat at the table with pen and paper, trying to think how to put it.

'I want this on record,' she wrote. 'I could kick myself in the head when I think of how he's led me on. I have been his patsy ten thousand times. As when that drunk crashed his Cub plane on the lake shore. At the coroner's jury he let me take the whole blame. He said he had instructed me when I was working for him never to take in any drunks. And this flier was drunk. He had nothing on but a T-shirt and Bermuda shorts and he was flying from Sacramento to Salt Lake City. At the inquest Pace said I had disobeyed his instructions. The same was true when the cook went haywire. She was a tramp. He never hires decent help. He cheated her on the bar bill and blamed me and she went after me with a meat cleaver. She disliked me because I criticized her for drinking at the bar in her one-piece white bathing suit with the dude guests. But he turned her loose on me. He hints that he did certain services for India. She would never have let him touch one single finger. He was too common for her. It can never be said about India that she was not a lady in every way. He thinks he is the greatest sack-artist in the world. He only loves horses, as a fact. He has no claims at all, oral or written, on this yellow house. I want you to have this over my signature. He was cruel to Pickle-Tits who was his first wife, and he's no better to the charming woman who is his present one. I don't know why she takes it. It must be despair.' Hattie said to herself, *I don't suppose I'd better send that.*

She was still angry. Her heart was knocking within; the deep pulses, as after a hot bath, beat at the back of her thighs. The air outside was dotted with transparent particles. The mountains were as red as furnace clinkers. The iris leaves were fan sticks – they stuck out like Jiggs's hair.

She always ended by looking out of the window at the desert and lake. *They drew you from yourself. But after they had drawn you, what did they do with you? It was too late to find out. I'll never know. I wasn't meant to. I'm not the type,* Hattie reflected. *Maybe something too cruel for women, young or old.*

So she stood up and, rising, she had the sensation that she had gradually become a container for herself. You get old, your heart, your liver, your lungs seem to expand in size, and the walls of the body give way outward, swelling, she thought, and you take the shape of an old jug, wider and wider toward the top. You swell up with tears and fat. She no longer even smelled to herself like a woman. Her face with its much-slept-upon skin was only faintly like her own – like a cloud that has changed.

It was a face. It became a ball of yarn. It had drifted open. It had scattered.

I was never one single thing anyway, she thought. Never my own. I was only loaned to myself.

But the thing wasn't over yet. And in fact she didn't know for certain that it was ever going to be over. You only had other people's word for it that death was such-and-such. How do I know? she asked herself challengingly. Her anger had sobered her for a little while. Now she was again drunk . . . *It was strange. It is strange. It may continue being strange.* She further thought, *I used to wish for death more than I do now. Because I didn't have anything at all. I changed when I got a roof of my own over me. And now? Do I have to go? I thought Marian loved me, but she already has a sister. And I thought Helen and Jerry would never desert me, but they've beat it. And now Pace has insulted me. They think I'm not going to make it.*

She went to the cupboard – she kept the bourbon bottle there; she drank less if each time she had to rise and open the cupboard door. And, as if she were being watched, she poured a drink and swallowed it.

The notion that in this emptiness someone saw her was connected with the other notion that she was being filmed from birth to death. That this was done for everyone. And afterward you could view your life. A hereafter movie.

Hattie wanted to see some of it now, and she sat down on the dogs'-paw cushions of her sofa and, with her knees far apart and a smile of yearning and of fright, she bent her round back, burned a cigarette at the corner of her mouth and saw – the Church of Saint Sulpice in Paris where her organ teacher used to bring her. It looked like country walls of stone, but rising high and leaning outward were towers. She was very young. She knew music. How she could ever have been so clever was beyond her. But she did know it. She could read all those notes. The sky was gray. After this she saw some entertaining things she liked to tell people about. She was a young wife. She was in Aix-les-Bains with her mother-in-law, and they played bridge in a mud bath with a British general and his aide. There were artificial waves in the swimming pool. She lost her bathing suit because it was a size too big. How did she get out? Ah, you got out of everything.

She saw her husband, James John Waggoner IV. They were snowbound together in New Hampshire. 'Jimmy, Jimmy, how can you fling a wife away?' she asked him. 'Have you forgotten love? Did I drink too much – did I bore you?' He had married again and had two children. He had gotten tried of her. And though he was a vain man with nothing to be vain about – no looks, not too much intelligence, nothing but an old Philadelphia family – she had loved him. She too had been a snob

45

about her Philadelphia connections. Give up the name of Waggoner? How could she? For this reason she had never married Wicks. 'How dare you,' she had said to Wicks, 'come without a shave in a dirty shirt and muck on you, come and ask me to marry! If you want to propose, go and clean up first.' But his dirt was only a pretext.

Trade Waggoner for Wicks? she asked herself again with a swing of her shoulders. She wouldn't think of it. Wicks was an excellent man. But he was a cowboy. Socially nothing. He couldn't even read. But she saw this on her film. They were in Athens Canyon, in a cratelike house, and she was reading aloud to him from *The Count of Monte Cristo.* He wouldn't let her stop. While walking to stretch her legs, she read, and he followed her about to catch each word. After all, he was very dear to her. Such a man! Now she saw him jump from his horse. They were living on the range, trapping coyotes. It was just the second gray of evening, cloudy, moments after the sun had gone down. There was an animal in the trap, and he went toward it to kill it. He wouldn't waste a bullet on the creatures but killed them with a kick, with his boot. And then Hattie saw that this coyote was all white – snarling teeth, white scruff. 'Wicks, he's white! White as a polar bear. You're not going to kill him, are you?' The animal flattened to the ground. He snarled and cried. He couldn't pull away because of the heavy trap. And Wicks killed him. What else could he have done? The white beast lay dead. The dust of Wicks's boots hardly showed on its head and jaws. Blood ran from the muzzle.

And now came something on Hattie's film she tried to shun. It was she herself who had killed her dog, Richie. Just as Rolfe and Pace had warned her, he was vicious, his brain was turned. She, because she was on the side of all dumb creatures, defended him when he bit the trashy woman Jacamares was living with. Perhaps if she had had Richie from a puppy he wouldn't have turned on her. When she got him he was already a year and a half old and she couldn't break him of his habits. But she thought that only she understood him. And Rolfe had warned her, 'You'll be sued, do you know that? The dog will take out after somebody smarter than that Jacamares's woman, and you'll be in for it.'

Hattie saw herself as she swayed her shoulders and said, 'Nonsense.'

But what fear she had felt when the dog went for her on the porch. Suddenly she could see, by his skull, by his eyes that he was evil. She screamed at him, 'Richie!' And what had she done to him? He had lain under the gas range all day growling and wouldn't come out. She tried

47

to urge him out with the broom, and he snatched it in his teeth. She pulled him out, and he left the stick and tore at her. Now, as the spectator of this, her eyes opened, beyond the pregnant curtain and the air-wave of marl dust, summer's snow, drifting over the water. 'Oh, my God! Richie!' Her thigh was snatched by his jaws. His teeth went through her skirt. She felt she would fall. Would she go down? Then the dog would rush at her throat – then black night, bad-odored mouth, the blood pouring from her neck, from torn veins. Her heart shriveled as the teeth went into her thigh, and she couldn't delay another second but took her kindling hatchet from the nail, strengthened her grip on the smooth wood, and hit the dog. She saw the blow. She saw him die at once. And then in fear and shame she hid the body. And at night she buried him in the yard. Next day she accused Jacamares. On him she laid the blame for the disappearance of her dog.

She stood up; she spoke to herself in silence, as was her habit. *God, what shall I do? I have taken life. I have lied. I have borne false witness. I have stalled. And now what shall I do? Nobody will help me.*

And suddenly she made up her mind that she should go and do what she had been putting off for weeks, namely, test herself with the car, and she slipped on her shoes and went outside. Lizards ran before her in the thirsty dust. She opened the hot, broad door of the car. She lifted her lame hand onto the wheel. With her right hand she reached far to the left and turned the wheel with all her might. Then she started the motor and tried to drive out of the yard. But she could not release the emergency brake with its rasplike rod. She reached with her good hand, the right, under the steering wheel and pressed her bosom on it and strained. No, she could not shift the gears and steer. She couldn't even reach down to the hand brake. The sweat broke out on her skin. Her efforts were too much. She was deeply wounded by the pain in her arm. The door of the car fell open again and she turned from the wheel and with her stiff legs hanging from the door she wept. What could she do now? And when she had wept over the ruin of her life she got out of the old car and went back to the house. She took the bourbon from the cupboard and picked up the ink bottle and a pad of paper and sat down to write her will.

'My Will,' she wrote, and sobbed to herself.

Since the death of India she had numberless times asked the question, To Whom? Who will get this when I die? She had unconsciously put people to the test to find out whether they were worthy. It made her more severe than before.

Now she wrote, 'I Harriet Simmons Waggoner, being of sound mind and not knowing what may be in store for me at the age of seventy-two (born 1885), living alone at Sego Desert Lake, instruct my lawyer, Harold Claiborne, Paiute County Court Building, to draw my last will and testament upon the following terms.'

She sat perfectly still now to hear from within who would be the lucky one, who would inherit the yellow house. For which she had waited. Yes, waited for India's death, choking on her bread because she was a rich woman's servant and whipping girl. But who had done for her, Hattie, what she had done for India? And who, apart from India, had ever held out a hand to her? Kindness, yes. Here and there people had been kind. But the word in her head was not kindness, it was succor. And who had given her that? *Succor*? Only India. If at least, next best after succor, someone had given her a shake and said, 'Stop stalling. Don't be such a slow, old, procrastinating sit-stiller.' Again, it was only India who had done her good. She had offered her succor. 'Het-tie!' said that drunken mask. 'Do you know what sloth is? Demn you! poky old demned thing!'

But I was waiting, Hattie realized. I was waiting, thinking, 'Youth is terrible, frightening. I will wait it out. And men? Men are cruel and strong. They want things I haven't got to give.' There were no kids in me, thought Hattie. *Not that I wouldn't have loved them, but such my nature was. And who can blame me for having it? My nature?*

She drank from an old-fashioned glass. There was no orange in it, no ice, no bitters or sugar, only the stinging, clear bourbon.

So then, she continued, looking at the dry sun-stamped dust and the last freckled flowers of red wild peach, *to live with Angus and his wife? And to have to hear a chapter from the Bible before breakfast? Once more in the house – not of a stranger, perhaps, but not far from it either?* In other houses, in someone else's house, to wait for mealtimes was her life-long punishment. She always felt it in the throat and stomach. And so she would again, and to the very end. However, she must think of someone to leave the house to.

And first of all she wanted to do right by her family. None of them had ever dreamed that she, Hattie, would ever have something to bequeath. Until a few years ago it had certainly looked as if she would die a pauper. So now she could keep her head up with the proudest of them. And, as this occurred to her, she actually lifted up her face with its broad nose and victorious eyes; if her hair had become shabby as onion roots, if, at the back, her head was round and bald as a newel post, what did that matter? Her heart experienced a childish glory, not yet tired of it after seventy-two years. She, too, had amounted to something. *I'll do some good by going*, she thought. *Now I believe I should leave it to, to . . .* She returned to the old point of struggle. She had decided

many times and many times changed her mind. She tried
to think, *Who would get the most out of this yellow house?*
It was a tearing thing to go through. If it had not been
the house but, instead, some brittle thing she could hold
in her hand, then her last action would be to throw and
smash it, and so the thing and she herself would be
demolished together. But it was vain to think such
thoughts. To whom should she leave it? Her brothers?
Not they. Nephews? One was a submarine commander.
The other was a bachelor in the State Department. Then
began the roll call of cousins. Merton? He owned an
estate in Connecticut. Anna? She had a face like a hot-
water bottle. That left Joyce, the orphaned daughter of
her cousin Wilfred. Joyce was the most likely heiress.
Hattie had already written to her and had her out to the
lake at Thanksgiving, two years ago. But this Joyce was
another odd one; over thirty, good, yes, but placid, run-
ning to fat, a scholar – ten years in Eugene, Oregon,
working for her degree. In Hattie's opinion this was only
another form of sloth. Nevertheless, Joyce yet hoped to
marry. Whom? Not Dr Stroud. He wouldn't. And still
Joyce had vague hopes. Hattie knew how that could be.
At least have a man she could argue with.

She was now more drunk than at any time since her
accident. Again she filled her glass. *Have ye eyes and see
not? Sleepers awake!*

Knees wide apart she sat in the twilight, thinking. Marian? Marian didn't need another house. Half Pint? She wouldn't know what to do with it. Brother Louis came up for consideration next. He was an old actor who had a church for the Indians at Athens Canyon. Hollywood stars of the silent days sent him their negligees; he altered them and wore them in the pulpit. The Indians loved his show. But when Billy Shawah blew his brains out after his two-week bender, they still tore his shack down and turned the boards inside out to get rid of his ghost. They had their old religion. No, not Brother Louis. He'd show movies in the yellow house to the tribe or make a nursery out of it for the Indian brats.

And now she began to consider Wicks. When last heard from he was south of Bishop, California, a handyman in a saloon off toward Death Valley. It wasn't she who heard from him but Pace. Herself, she hadn't actually seen Wicks since – how low she had sunk then! – she had kept the hamburger stand on Route 158. The little lunchroom had supported them both. Wicks hung around on the end stool, rolling cigarettes (she saw it on the film). Then there was a quarrel. Things had been going from bad to worse. He'd begun to grouse now about this and now about that. He beefed about the food, at last. She saw and heard him. 'Hat,' he said, 'I'm good and tired of hamburger.' 'Well, what do you think

I eat?' she said with that round, defiant movement of her shoulders which she herself recognized as characteristic (*me all over*, she thought). But he opened the cash register and took out thirty cents and crossed the street to the butcher's and brought back a steak. He threw it on the griddle. 'Fry it,' he said. She did, and watched him eat.

And when he was through she could bear her rage no longer. 'Now,' she said, 'you've had your meat. Get out. Never come back.' She kept a pistol under the counter. She picked it up, cocked it, pointed it at his heart. 'If you ever come in that door again, I'll kill you,' she said.

She saw it all. *I couldn't bear to fall so low*, she thought, *to be slave to a shiftless cowboy*.

Wicks said, 'Don't do that, Hat. Guess I went too far. You're right.'

'You'll never have a chance to make it up,' she cried. 'Get out!'

On that cry he disappeared, and since then she had never seen him.

'Wicks, dear,' she said. 'Please! I'm sorry. Don't condemn me in your heart. Forgive me. I hurt myself in my evil. I always had a thick idiot head. I was born with a thick head.'

Again she wept, for Wicks. She was too proud. A snob. Now they might have lived together in this house, old friends, simple and plain.

She thought, *He really was my good friend.*

But what would Wicks do with a house like this, alone, if he was alive and survived her? He was too wiry for soft beds or easy chairs.

And she was the one who had said stiffly to India, 'I'm a Christian person. I do not bear a grudge.'

Ah yes, she said to herself. *I have caught myself out too often. How long can this go on?* And she began to think, or try to think, of Joyce, her cousin's daughter Joyce was like herself, a woman alone, getting on in years, clumsy. Probably never been laid. Too bad. She would have given much, now, to succor Joyce.

But it seemed to her now that that too, the succor, had been a story. First you heard the pure story. Then you heard the impure story. Both stories. She had paid out years, now to one shadow, now to another shadow.

Joyce would come here to the house. She had a little income and could manage. She would live as Hattie had lived, alone. Here she would rot, start to drink, maybe, and day after day read, day after day sleep. See how beautiful it was here? It burned you out. How empty! It turned you into ash.

How can I doom a younger person to the same life? asked Hattie. It's for somebody like me. When I was younger it wasn't right. But now it is, exactly. Only I fit in here. It was made for my old age, to spend my last years peacefully. If I hadn't let Jerry make me drunk that night – if I hadn't sneezed! Because of this arm, I'll have to live with Angus. My heart will break there away from my only home.

She was now very drunk, and she said to herself, *Take what God brings. He gives no gifts unmixed. He makes loans.*

She resumed her letter of instructions to lawyer Claiborne: 'Upon the following terms,' she wrote a second time. 'Because I have suffered much. Because I only lately received what I have to give away, I can't bear it.' The drunken blood was soaring to her head. But her hand was clear enough. She wrote, 'It is too soon! Too soon! Because I do not find it in my heart to care for anyone as I would wish. Being cast off and lonely, and doing no harm where I am. Why should it be? This breaks my heart. In addition to everything else, why must I worry about this, which I must leave? I am tormented out of my mind. Even though by my own fault I have put myself into this position. And I am not ready to give up on this. No, not yet. And so I'll tell you what, I leave this property, land, house, garden, and water rights, to Hattie Simmons Waggoner. Me! I realize this is bad and wrong. Not possible. Yet it is the only thing I really wish to do, so may God have mercy on my soul.'

How could that happen? She studied what she had written (and finally acknowledged there was no alternative). 'I'm drunk,' she said, 'and don't know what I'm doing. I'll die, and end. Like India. Dead as that lilac bush.'

Then she thought that there was a beginning, and a middle. She shrank from the last term. She began once more – a beginning. After that, there was the early middle, then middle middle, late middle middle, quite late middle. In fact the middle is all I know. The rest is just a rumor.

Only tonight I can't give the house away. I'm drunk and so I need it. And tomorrow, she promised herself, I'll think again. I'll work it out, for sure.

1. MARTIN LUTHER KING, JR. · *Letter from Birmingham Jail*
2. ALLEN GINSBERG · *Television Was a Baby Crawling Toward That Deathchamber*
3. DAPHNE DU MAURIER · *The Breakthrough*
4. DOROTHY PARKER · *The Custard Heart*
5. *Three Japanese Short Stories*
6. ANAÏS NIN · *The Veiled Woman*
7. GEORGE ORWELL · *Notes on Nationalism*
8. GERTRUDE STEIN · *Food*
9. STANISLAW LEM · *The Three Electroknights*
10. PATRICK KAVANAGH · *The Great Hunger*
11. DANILO KIŠ · *The Legend of the Sleepers*
12. RALPH ELLISON · *The Black Ball*
13. JEAN RHYS · *Till September Petronella*
14. FRANZ KAFKA · *Investigations of a Dog*
15. CLARICE LISPECTOR · *Daydream and Drunkenness of a Young Lady*
16. RYSZARD KAPUŚCIŃSKI · *An Advertisement for Toothpaste*
17. ALBERT CAMUS · *Create Dangerously*
18. JOHN STEINBECK · *The Vigilante*
19. FERNANDO PESSOA · *I Have More Souls Than One*
20. SHIRLEY JACKSON · *The Missing Girl*
21. *Four Russian Short Stories*
22. ITALO CALVINO · *The Distance of the Moon*
23. AUDRE LORDE · *The Master's Tools Will Never Dismantle the Master's House*
24. LEONORA CARRINGTON · *The Skeleton's Holiday*
25. WILLIAM S. BURROUGHS · *The Finger*

26. SAMUEL BECKETT · *The End*

27. KATHY ACKER · *New York City in 1979*

28. CHINUA ACHEBE · *Africa's Tarnished Name*

29. SUSAN SONTAG · *Notes on 'Camp'*

30. JOHN BERGER · *The Red Tenda of Bologna*

31. FRANÇOISE SAGAN · *The Gigolo*

32. CYPRIAN EKWENSI · *Glittering City*

33. JACK KEROUAC · *Piers of the Homeless Night*

34. HANS FALLADA · *Why Do You Wear a Cheap Watch?*

35. TRUMAN CAPOTE · *The Duke in His Domain*

36. SAUL BELLOW · *Leaving the Yellow House*

37. KATHERINE ANNE PORTER · *The Cracked Looking-Glass*

38. JAMES BALDWIN · *Dark Days*

39. GEORGES SIMENON · *Letter to My Mother*

40. WILLIAM CARLOS WILLIAMS · *Death the Barber*

41. BETTY FRIEDAN · *The Problem that Has No Name*

42. FEDERICO GARCÍA LORCA · *The Dialogue of Two Snails*

43. YUKO TSUSHIMA · *Of Dogs and Walls*

44. JAVIER MARÍAS · *Madame du Deffand and the Idiots*

45. CARSON MCCULLERS · *The Haunted Boy*

46. JORGE LUIS BORGES · *The Garden of Forking Paths*

47. ANDY WARHOL · *Fame*

48. PRIMO LEVI · *The Survivor*

49. VLADIMIR NABOKOV · *Lance*

50. WENDELL BERRY · *Why I Am Not Going to Buy a Computer*